Picking on Percy

by

Catherine MacPhail

Illustrated by Karen Donnelly

You do not need to read this page – just get on with the book!

First published in 2000 in Great Britain by
Barrington Stoke Ltd
www.barringtonstoke.co.uk

This edition published 2006

ISBN-10: 1-842994-12-3
ISBN-13: 978-1-84299-412-2

Printed in Great Britain by Bell & Bain Ltd

MEET THE AUTHOR - CATHERINE MACPHAIL

What is your favourite animal?
Elephant
What is your favourite boy's name?
David
What is your favourite girl's name?
Sarah
What is your favourite food?
Mussels
What is your favourite music?
Mary Black
What is your favourite hobby?
Writing

MEET THE ILLUSTRATOR - KAREN DONNELLY

What is your favourite animal?
Woodlice!
What is your favourite boy's name?
Laurie
What is your favourite girl's name?
Jean
What is your favourite food?
Sausages and runny eggs
What is your favourite music?
Beck
What is your favourite hobby?
Drawing and printmaking

Contents

Chapter 1
Picking on Percy

Percy was asleep in the maths lesson again. In fact, he was snoring. Mrs Hume, the teacher, was slightly deaf so she hadn't heard him yet.

I looked across at my pal, Sammy Boy, and winked at him. Then I turned my gaze on Percy. Sammy Boy smiled. Percy asleep again? This was too good a chance to miss.

"Go for it, Shawn," he mouthed at me silently.

We lifted the lids of our desks and at exactly the same second let them drop.

Percy let out a terrific yell. Mrs Hume heard that all right. She jumped three feet in the air and let out a terrific yell of her own.

"Percy Brown! What do you think you are playing at?" she bellowed.

Percy swallowed. "Please, Miss, it wasn't my fault," he replied.

I burst out laughing. I couldn't help it. You simply had to laugh at that high-pitched nasal whine of Percy's. It sounded as if someone was strangling a cat. If I was Percy, I thought, I'd learn sign language. I'd stay silent and never open my mouth again.

"It wasn't his fault, Miss," I said, in exactly the same voice as Percy's.

This time it was Sammy Boy who burst out laughing. He thought I did a brilliant take-off of Percy's voice. "The lid of my desk slipped out of my hand. That's what woke Percy up."

Mrs Hume almost had a fit. "Woke him up?" She glared at Percy. "Were you asleep again, Percy?"

Now Percy glared at me. I don't know why. I was completely innocent. I had told her it wasn't his fault, hadn't I? Some people are never grateful.

He had the cheek to come up to me in the playground later. "One day you're going to regret picking on me, Shawn Russell," he whined.

"One day you're going to regret picking on me, Shawn Russell," I repeated in just the same whining voice. "I don't think!" I added, but this time I used my own voice which was a big improvement on Percy's.

I mean, picking on Percy was such a laugh. He walked right into it. As I said to Sammy Boy, "Picking on Percy's the best fun you can have without a football."

For a start, Percy's the smallest boy in the class. He's always got dribbles down his blazer. You can practically tell what he had for his breakfast everyday and today it was porridge.

And then there are those trainers of his. Cheap, plastic ones. Everybody laughs at them. Everybody else has designer trainers like mine. Honestly, I'd die if my mother made me go to school wearing Percy's trainers.

And worst of all, the boy hates football! He says he prefers reading. I ask you. Percy deserves all he gets. Imagine anybody with any sense preferring a book to football?

The bell rang and Percy strode off, trying to look cool. Unfortunately, he tripped over the laces on his cheap trainers and went flying down onto the ground. I was still laughing as I went into my next class.

That was when I bumped into Laura. Now, Laura really fancies me. Not that I blame her for that. I'm the best football player in the school. A lot of the girls fancy me. Except Rebecca, who's the one I really like. But the sad thing is, Laura is nothing to look at. In fact, she's just about the ugliest girl in the school.

"Hello, Shawn." Laura smiled and simpered and tried to flutter her eyelashes. She only managed to make her eyes water.

"Goodbye, Laura," I answered and brushed past her.

"She really fancies you," Sammy Boy said with a giggle.

I didn't think it was anything to laugh at.

"I wish SHE fancied me," I said, pointing over to the lovely Rebecca. She never looked in my direction, except when she wanted to sneer at me. Oh, well, it was her loss. She was a snob. And if there's anything I hate, it's a snob.

Chapter 2
Magic Mo

That day on the way home from school, I decided to pop into the amusement arcade. Now, that was fate. I'd hardly ever done that before. So why did I go that particular day? I just don't know.

And who do you think was there too? Percy. He was staring hard at a machine right at the back. A machine I'd never seen before.

I tiptoed up behind him and gave him the fright of his pathetic little life.

"So what sort of machine has got you hooked then?" I pushed him aside.

"It's called Magic Mo," Percy answered in his nasal voice.

The face of Magic Mo stared out at me, like a kindly genie. He had a long beard and he was wearing a turban. Lights danced around his head and his eyes sparkled. It was hard to look away from those eyes.

"Magic Mo can make you become the person you would most like to be," I heard Percy say. But it seemed his voice was somewhere far in the distance. "I'm going to put my money in and see what happens," Percy added.

I dragged my eyes away from Magic Mo. Then I began to laugh.

"And who do you most want to be, Percy son? David Beckham? Bart Simpson? Or maybe ... you'd like to be me?"

Percy pushed the money into the slot. "That would be my worst nightmare!" he snapped.

This was the boldest Percy had ever been with me.

"And do you know what my worst nightmare would be, Percy boy? To be you!" I told him.

And that's when it happened. The machine went bananas. Lights began to flash and explode all around Magic Mo's head. The machine wailed and screeched. It seemed as if Magic Mo was going to leap

from the screen. I thought his smile grew
wider. I thought he laughed.

My hair stood on end, I'm almost sure of
it.

Then, just as suddenly as it had begun, it
finished. The machine settled down to a
steady hum and the light went out of Magic
Mo's eyes. He was smiling in his kindly way
again.

13

"Percy! What happened there?"

But when I looked around for Percy, he had gone. This was just as well for him. I was about to get him for talking back to me. So I went home.

Then the nightmare started.

****

I knocked on my front door because I'd forgotten my key again. Mum opened it but not very wide.

"Hi, Mum," I said, and I tried to step inside. She held out her hand to stop me.

"Mum?" she asked, in a puzzled voice. "Why are you calling me Mum?"

My Mum's a joker. She's always laughing and singing opera. So I laughed.

"Well, I'm your son, aren't I?" I said. But my voice sounded funny. I began to think I had a cold coming on. "I'm your beloved Shawn," I reminded her. I was her only child.

I smiled at her but she didn't smile back. You do expect your own Mum to know who you are. But she still looked really puzzled.

"Honey, I'm home!" I almost sang it. She loved it when I almost sang.

"Who are you, then? Shawn's been home for ten minutes."

And do you know, she was right, because just then someone who looked just like me came out of the living room and stood behind her.

But it couldn't be me behind her, because I was out here on the pavement.

So what was happening?

"I know who you are!" my Mum said suddenly. "You're that Percy Brown. What are you doing here?"

"Did you say ... Percy Brown?" I was beginning to get a really bad feeling about this.

"You get away home, Percy!" And with that my Mum slammed my own front door in my face.

It was at that point that my heart almost stopped beating. Because there, in the glass panel of the door, I could see my reflection. And what I could see ... was not me at all but PERCY!

So that was why my Mum had slammed the door. I had dribbles down my blazer, plastic trainers, the lot.

I began to shake. Maybe I did have a cold coming on. Just at that moment, the door was pulled open and there was the someone who looked just like me.

"I'm still me, Percy, inside!" he said. "I just look like you. It's a real mix-up."

"I know," I said bitterly. "I don't understand what's happened either but somewhere deep down in this body of yours, I'm still Shawn."

He was shaking too. "I went home and my mother wouldn't let me in either. She thought I was you. In fact, she gave me an awful telling off for bullying her son, Percy."

"I do not bully you. I only pick on you a bit," I said, quite offended.

It was very strange explaining these things to someone who was me, Shawn, on the outside.

"Bullying, teasing, it's the same thing," he said.

"I don't want to be you," I told Percy in that awful voice of his.

"I don't want to be you, Shawn, either. Your mother keeps singing to me."

My mother called from the kitchen. "Shawn, come along. Your pizza's ready."

Pizza. My favourite. My mother makes a great pizza. I almost stepped inside the door until I realised she wasn't talking to me. I was Percy.

"I'd better go," the boy who was the real Percy whispered. Then he turned back. "I hate to tell you," he hesitated, "but at my house, this is egg and chips night."

The front door was shut in my face. Once more I was staring at my reflection in the glass panel.

I still looked like Percy. PERCY!

This had to be a nightmare.

Chapter 3
Baby from Hell

I began walking. I didn't know where I was going and I didn't care. What was I going to do? I had never been so scared in my life. How could this happen? Who could I confide in? Who would believe me?

Someone was shouting behind me. "Percy! Percy Brown!" I took no notice and kept on walking.

Suddenly, I was grabbed by the scruff of the neck and almost lifted off the ground.

"You're late for your paper round. Again!" It was Mr Harkins, the newsagent. He dragged me into the shop.

Paper round? Percy had a paper round? Mr Harkins slung a bag overflowing with evening papers round my neck. It was so heavy I choked. He gave me a push that sent me flying against the wall.

"If you're late one more time I'll be taking money off your wages."

His face was so close to mine I could smell his breath. It was awful, as if he'd been eating rotten eggs. I could see the hairs in his nose. They kept fluttering every time he breathed. He was one ugly man.

I was going to tell him where he could stick his papers, but by the way he was shaking me I didn't think he was in any mood to listen.

"But where do I deliver them?" I asked as he was shoving me out of the shop.

"Is there something wrong with your memory?" He pointed a dirty-nailed finger at the three tower blocks at the top of the hill. "Up there!" he snapped.

Would you believe that not one of those tower blocks had a lift that worked?

This nightmare was getting worse by the minute.

By the time I'd finished delivering the papers my legs felt like jelly. I was so hungry that Percy's mother's egg and chips was sounding better by the minute.

What else could I do? Where else could I go?

I went home to Percy's. And do you know where Percy lived? Yes. On the tenth floor of one of those tower blocks! We teased him about it at school.

At least, I was thinking as I knocked on Percy's door, things couldn't get much worse. Then I met the Baby from Hell and knew that they could.

The door was opened by Mrs Brown. "Hello, dear, you're late tonight. I've kept your egg and chips hot in the oven for you."

In her arms was the most frightening looking baby boy I had ever seen in my life.

He was caked in dried-up mashed potato. As soon as he saw me he screeched with delight and pelted me with a handful

of potato. He must have been keeping it just for me. Then he launched himself at me like a rocket.

"This baby just loves his big brother," Mrs Brown giggled. "Don't you, Archie?"

Archie! She had called one of her sons Percy and the other Archie. Did this woman not like children?

Archie's chubby fingers were all over my face, exploring my mouth, clawing at my hair. It was disgusting. I wanted to scream, *Get this baby off me!*

But who would listen? Instead, I sat at the table with Archie on my knee and waited while Mrs Brown fetched my dinner from the kitchen. I looked at the plate of dried-up egg and greasy chips that she put in front of me. It must have been in the oven for a long, long time.

"Come to Mummy, Archie," she said, taking the baby from me. "Let Percy enjoy his tea."

Enjoy? Was the woman mad? She tried to pull Archie from me, but he didn't want to go. He twined his fingers round my hair and held on fast. She had quite a struggle getting him off me and when she did my hair was covered in mashed potato.

I looked at the plate for a long time. All I could think of was my mother's pizza. I could almost picture the real Percy, sitting in front of my TV, stuffed with my favourite food and contented. Even my mother's constant singing would be a small price to pay for that.

Suddenly, I felt two pairs of eyes boring into me. I looked up and blinked. Was I seeing double? Two identical little girls were standing in front of me, Percy's little sisters. I had known that Percy's sisters were twins, but I hadn't known that they looked so much alike.

Morag and Agnes. I knew their names because they were emblazoned on the necklaces they were both wearing. Morag and Agnes! That was almost as bad as Percy and Archie.

"Tell us a story!" Morag demanded.

"You're brilliant at telling stories, Percy," Agnes insisted.

Me? Tell a story? I couldn't tell a story to save my life. I looked over at Mrs Brown for help. The baby looked as though he was ready to throw himself at me again.

"Just don't make it too scary, Percy," Mrs Brown said.

So I told them a story about the wicked wizard from Wales. Well, I don't know where that story came from. Somewhere deep inside me that was Percy. It was a great story. Even I was dying to know the end.

That was brilliant, I thought as soon as I'd finished.

"You always tell brilliant stories, Percy," said Morag.

"You're the best big brother in the world."

And with that Agnes threw herself at me and planted a big, wet kiss on my cheek. Yuck! Poor Percy. Did he have to suffer this every night? I was beginning to feel sorry for him.

I fell into Percy's bed that night. I was worn out and I have to admit a wee bit scared.

How had this happened? It had to be a bad dream. A nightmare. That was the only way to explain it.

I was going to wake up tomorrow, safe and sound, in my own bed.

Chapter 4
I'm Not Percy!

"Wake up, Percy. It's time to get up."

It was pitch-black and the alarm was going off. Percy's Dad had just come in from the night shift and was shaking me.

"Time to get up? I've only just got to bed." I looked at the clock. It was six o'clock.

"You're going to be late for your paper round."

"Another paper round? In the middle of the night? Have I gone mad?"

Mr Brown nodded. "Well, I think you're mad, Percy," he said. "And all because you've got to have those designer trainers. There's nothing wrong with the ones you've got."

I couldn't believe it. Percy was working like a slave to save up for designer trainers, just like mine.

I dragged myself out of bed and headed for the newsagent. Mr Harkins was waiting for me at the door of the shop. He grabbed me by the collar.

"I've had a complaint about you, Percy Brown," he said, shaking me as if I was a rag doll. "You let Mrs Jones' Doberman eat her evening paper."

"It was either that or the dog was going to eat *me*," I protested.

Mr Harkins didn't seem to understand. Instead he spat out crossly, "Next time you'd better let it eat you. This is your last chance, Brown."

None of the lifts were working again, and by the time I got to school, my legs were aching. No wonder Percy hated PE. He got enough exercise delivering those papers.

I fell asleep in maths.

And do you know what? My pal, Sammy Boy, woke me up with the old 'slam down the desk' trick. Mrs Hume went crazy! She told me if I fell asleep again in her class she was reporting me to the headmaster.

In the playground, I tried to explain to my best friend what was happening to me.

"Sammy Boy, don't you recognise me? I'm not really Percy Brown."

I wish Percy didn't have this horrible voice. At once Sammy Boy began to mimic me. Of course he didn't believe me. I looked like Percy. Who else could I be?

"Who do you think you are then? Superman? Terminator 3? And by the way," he said grabbing me by the collar, "nobody ever calls me Sammy Boy, except my pal, Shawn."

I began to get excited. "But that's who I really am," I told him. "Shawn!"

Sammy Boy began to laugh. He shouted across the playground, "Hey, Shawn, come on over here and help me teach this wimp a lesson."

Across the playground, leaning against the wall, was Shawn. Me. But inside I knew that Percy was trapped in there.

Percy was lucky. He had the best deal. He had a mother who could cook. And seeing myself from this angle, I realised I was pretty good looking as well. (Except for my nose. That was a bit big, but nobody ever remarked on it. I'm a bit big too.)

Sammy Boy kept shaking me. I'd had enough by this time. I plucked his hands from my collar. "You're not going to teach me a lesson. You want to be ashamed of yourself. I'm a lot smaller than you are."

Sammy Boy was shocked. Percy had never had the nerve to talk back to him before.

"So what are you going to do about it, birdbrain?" he said. "Hit me one on the jaw or kick me on the shins? You just try it."

"I'm getting angry now, Sammy Boy," I said.

Sammy Boy thought this was really funny. He repeated what I'd said in exactly the same voice, "I'm getting angry now, Sammy Boy."

That did it! I lifted my foot and kicked him as hard as I could on the shins.

While he was dancing about in agony, I shouted, "I can't help the way I talk. I've got something wrong with my nose."

Too late, I remembered how big Sammy Boy was and as his fist came racing towards me, I knew that in a few seconds I really would have something wrong with my nose.

Chapter 5
Nightmare Time

I came to with blood gushing from my nose. The real Percy was standing over me.

"I want to be myself again. I don't like being Percy," I said.

"Well, you did kick him on the shins first."

This was Percy, the real Percy speaking, who only looked like me. And he was sticking up for Sammy Boy! I could hardly believe it.

"Hey, you're supposed to stick up for me!" I told him, as he was helping me up. "After all, we're both in this mix-up together."

Sammy Boy was nowhere to be seen.

"Did you take my medicine this morning?" the real Percy whispered. "I'm supposed to use a nasal inhaler every morning. I've got to have it. It makes my voice sound better."

"A nasal inhaler?" I repeated. "Percy son, you are falling to bits."

Just then, the real Percy was pushed aside. There, standing over me, was the lovely Rebecca.

"You buzz off, Shawn Russell," she snapped at Percy. "You're nothing but a bully. Come on, Percy," she said to me, "I'll take you to the nurse."

I thought it was a bit unfair that she should snap at Percy, even though she did think it was me. After all, it was Sammy Boy who had punched me.

"Actually, Shawn was helping me up," I told her.

"You're too nice, Percy," she said to me as she dragged me off, all concerned. I decided to enjoy the moment. Rebecca had never been nice to me before. Even if she thought it was Percy she was being nice to.

The headmaster was waiting for me at the nurse's office. "I believe you were rather violent to Samuel," he said.

Now I knew where Sammy Boy had raced off to.

"He punched me, sir." I pointed to my nose which was bleeding all over the corridor.

"Only after you kicked him, I believe."

Well, I couldn't deny that. "He's always picking on me, sir." I sounded really pathetic.

"I know you've had a lot of provocation, Percy." Our headmaster loves using big words which none of us understand. "But you must never use violence to defend yourself," he said.

At that moment, all I wanted was to get to the nurse. I sniffed and dripped more blood, but the headmaster did not seem to notice.

"Samuel and Shawn will both be punished for giving you a hard time."

Both! Poor old Shawn – Percy, I mean! He was going to be punished and he hadn't done anything.

"But I have to acknowledge," the headmaster went on, using the big words again, "that I believe Shawn is a changed boy. He has been so helpful today at school. And guess what? He's just joined the school choir.

Something we've been asking him to do for a long time. He has a marvellous voice."

I began to choke. Sing in the school choir! Shawn? Me? The coolest dude in the school. What was Percy trying to do to my image? Well, two could play at that game.

I said, in Percy's nasal whine, "I'll try to be a changed boy as well, sir. Put me down for the football team."

I'd like to see Percy's face when he hears about that!

Chapter 6
Worst Day of my Life

That day was the worst day of my life. I'd never realised how much Percy got picked on. Just because he was small. Just because he was skinny. Just because there were dribbles all down his blazer. And just because he always sounded as if someone was trying to strangle him. To add to my misery, I kept tripping over those blinking shoelaces!

I plodded home deep in thought. Home. Where was home? It seemed I had no choice but to go back to Percy's, and the Baby from Hell. I was so deep in thought, I walked straight into the arms of Mr Harkins.

This time he didn't grab me by the collar or the scruff of my neck. This time he lifted me by the ears into his shop. I'd had enough. I wriggled and I squirmed and I yelled.

"Put me down!"

"You're a useless, no-good little wimp of a boy!" Mr Harkins yelled back at me. "And if you don't behave yourself, you're fired."

"You don't have to fire me," I shouted. "I quit. I don't need designer trainers that much."

That took him completely by surprise. His false teeth began to quiver. I thought they were about to fall out. Disgusting.

I decided to make a quick exit from the shop.

"Let me tell you this, boy," Mr Harkins called after me. "You'll never deliver papers in this town again."

"Good!" I shouted back at him.

****

When I told Percy's mother she was thrilled.

"I'm so glad. I never wanted you to work for that horrible man."

Baby Archie celebrated by throwing up all over me. And the story I told Morag and Agnes that night was the best ever. Now all I had to do was tell Percy.

You would think he might have been pleased. Instead he went bananas. He stamped about the playground like an idiot.

"I had nearly saved up enough money for those trainers. And you've ruined everything," shouted the real Percy.

"You don't need them. I promise. I'll never wear mine again," I told him.

Percy glared at me. "I know you won't, pal," he sneered, "because your Mum took me shopping yesterday and I made her buy me the plastic kind. I said they were all the fashion in school now."

I was totally shocked. What a rotten thing to do.

"You and your big hooter are going to be sorry for that!" I yelled at him.

No one had ever commented on my big nose. No one had ever dared. So I couldn't believe what I'd just said. Here I was, insulting myself.

I could see people in the playground begin to snigger.

That was the last straw. I jumped on him and down we went in a heap.

"I can't hit you," he kept saying. "You're a lot smaller than me."

"Don't let that stop you," I said. And I landed a punch right between his eyes.

I would have landed another, but just then I was lifted off, still struggling, by the headmaster himself.

Chapter 7
Nobody Loves Shawn

"Percy, Percy, Percy! Why are you behaving like this?"

I was sitting in the headmaster's office listening to one of his lectures. I'd had them many times before. But I knew that Percy hadn't.

"You're just not yourself," he said.

I know I'm not myself, I wanted to shout at him. But he'd never believe me.

"And don't blame Shawn," he said as I opened my mouth to speak. "There were people standing nearby who have told me that he refused to hit you back because you're smaller than he is."

Wonderful! I felt like punching the real Percy again.

The headmaster gave me a stern letter to take home to Mrs Brown. But when school was over I didn't go back to Percy's house. Instead, I found myself trailing back to my own house. I decided I'd had enough of this, enough of being Percy. I wanted to be myself again.

I could hear my mother singing as I walked up the street. I'd never really noticed what a nice voice she had. Out of tune, yes, but right at this minute it sounded heavenly to me. Now she could sing at me 24 hours a day if she wanted. If she would just believe me and help me find a way to get back into my own body.

Then another voice joined hers, singing with her. Shawn's voice. My voice.

I tiptoed to the front window and peeked inside. There they were, my mother and her son singing together. Her dream had come true. I'd never seen her look happier.

What was the point of trying to make her believe me? She preferred the new Shawn. Everybody did. Percy had been inside my body for three days and he'd turned me into a perfectly likeable boy.

And what had I done for Percy? I'd lost him his job. I'd got him into trouble at school. And now I was going back to his house with a warning letter from the headmaster. I'd never felt so miserable in all my life.

In the end I didn't knock on the door. I turned and went back to Percy's house. On the way I met Mrs Jones and her Doberman. He was hungry again so I gave him the headmaster's letter. He ate it in one gulp.

When I walked in, the Baby from Hell threw himself at me, screaming with joy.

"That baby just loves you," Percy's Mum said happily.

"You're the best big brother in the world," Morag and Agnes said together.

But it was Percy they loved.

Not me.

Nobody loved Shawn.

****

I stood in the playground the next day on my own. Miserable.

"I want to go back to being myself," a voice said.

I looked up. The real Percy was standing there, looking as miserable as I felt.

"Why should you want to go back?" I asked him. "You've got it made. My mother spoils her only son. Even if she doesn't ever shut up with the singing. And she's a good cook."

My mouth watered at the thought of her pizza.

"I miss my family," Percy said. "I miss the baby."

"I wish he'd miss me sometimes," I said. "Especially when he throws that porridge."

And do you know what happened then? Suddenly, we were both laughing.

People began to look up at us, puzzled. Rebecca looked ready to run over and rescue Percy from the evil Shawn. I began to wonder if Rebecca fancied him. Well, if I had to stay as Percy that might make up for it.

I saw Sammy Boy too, watching us. He looked baffled. I knew then I'd never be friends with Sammy Boy again. We had nothing in common.

"I'll never laugh at your dribbles again," I told Percy. "Now I know how hard it is to avoid them."

Percy laughed. "He always manages to splat you just when you're going out the door."

We were both silent for a moment. We were both thinking the same thing. We both wanted home, to be back in our own bodies, living our own lives.

But how?

Suddenly, I had a brilliant idea. "The amusement arcade. Magic Mo! You put the money in and the machine went bananas. Totally crazy!"

"That must be it," Percy said. "We've got to go back there and do everything again, exactly as before."

It had to work. I'd never prayed so hard. It just had to work.

Chapter 8
Game Over

There was the machine, humming softly in the very back corner of the amusement arcade. Magic Mo. He looked helpful and kind with his gentle, smiling eyes. It looked for all the world like a perfectly normal machine you'd find in any arcade.

The idea that there could be anything magical about the machine seemed crazy.

"We have to try," Percy said.

He felt the same way I did. Unsure. Afraid.

"Put the money in," I told him.

He slipped the coins in the slot and we waited. For a minute or two nothing happened.

I held my breath.

Then, all at once, Magic Mo came to life. His eyes lit up. The lights flashed round his head. They exploded. Bells rang. The machine wailed and screeched. Magic Mo seemed about to leap from the screen.

I looked at Percy. Nothing had changed. It wasn't going to work. For one awful moment I was sure it wasn't going to work.

I closed my eyes and prayed. *Please. Please. Let me be me again.*

I didn't open them until all the wailing and screeching had stopped and Magic Mo was humming softly once again. The first thing I saw was my blazer.

MY blazer. No dribbles. No porridge. No mashed potato. It HAD worked! I yelled at the top of my voice. "Percy! I'm me again!"

But Percy wasn't there.

He was waiting for me outside the arcade. Sitting on the step with his head in his hands. His face was chalk white. "Oh, Shawn. I was really scared then."

I hauled him to his feet. "But it worked," I said. It was wonderful having my own voice back again. I did feel like singing.

"Do you know what I hated most about being you?" Percy said.

I began to laugh. "How could you hate anything about being me?"

"You couldn't tell a story to save your life," he went on.

"That was the best thing about being you, Percy. You're brilliant at telling stories."

We began walking along the road. "You are a good singer, you know," Percy told me. "I think you might end up a pop star or something. Maybe you could get into a boy band."

Now, I'd never thought about that. To me singing always meant opera. Fat men belting out songs at the top of their voices in a different language. But a pop star. That was different.

"Of course," Percy went on, pointing at my nose, "you'd have to do something about the size of that hooter."

Percy roared with laughter. I chased him down the street and caught him. I put my hands round his neck and pretended to strangle him. But we were laughing, giggling. Anyone seeing us together would think we were friends.

The truth is I'll never be friends with Percy. I mean, being friends might mean he'd invite me to his home and the Baby from Hell might vomit on me again. No chance!

But I'll never pick on him again. I know now Percy has enough to put up with.

We said goodbye. Percy was going home to his house, his mother's rotten cooking, his sisters who loved his stories and the baby who adored him.

I was going back to my Singing Mamma!

As if he'd read my thoughts, Percy reached into my top pocket and pulled something out. It was a set of ear plugs.

"Here, use them," he said. "They work great."

I watched him walk away. He tripped over his laces again. This time I didn't laugh. Well, not a lot.

Percy turned back at the corner and waved. "By the way," he shouted, "I'd better tell you. You've got a date on Saturday night."

I beamed back at him, "Rebecca?"

He shook his head. "No, with Laura actually!"

Then he was off, running and laughing. Laura, just about the ugliest girl in the school. He was a wee devil that Percy.

"I'll get you for that, Percy," I shouted after him.

But I knew that I wouldn't. Anyway, in a way I already had. Just wait till he finds out about the ten mile sponsored hike I've put him down for at the weekend!

Barrington Stoke would like to thank all its readers for commenting on the manuscript before publication and in particular:

Michael Addison
Liz Cochrane
Rachel Fenwick
Gareth Franklin
Nicholas Good
Rosanna Hall
Andrew Hare
Charlotte Hawkes
Azmal Hussein
Svetlana Kondakova
Sean Lassuer
Michael McLeod
Brena Pollitt
Esther, Tim, Josh, Emily and James Ryley
Sophie Suominen
Alison Waugh

Become a Consultant!

Would you like to give us feedback on our titles before they are published? Contact us at the email address or website below – we'd love to hear from you!

E-mail: info@barringtonstoke.co.uk
Website: www.barringtonstoke.co.uk

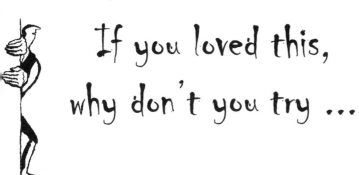

If you loved this, why don't you try ...

Get That Ghost To Go!
by Catherine MacPhail

Duncan doesn't know what's hit him when Dean's ghost begins to follow him everywhere. Dean chases dogs and upsets the teachers but no one else can see him. So Duncan gets the blame! How on earth can Duncan and his best friends get that ghost to go?

You can order *Get That Ghost To Go!* directly from our website at www.barringtonstoke.co.uk

If you loved this, why don't you try ...

Problems with a Python
by Jeremy Strong

What's one metre long, and doesn't belong in school?

Adam is looking after his friend's pet python. But he thinks snakes are boring ... until he takes her to school, and she escapes! Can Adam find the snake before things get s-s-s-seriously silly?